North Pole

To Amanda, Neil, Otis and Leah
—J.S.

For my good friends
Jim and Raechele
— T.W.

tiger tales
an imprint of ME Media, LLC
202 Old Ridgefield Road, Wilton, CT 06897
Published in the United States 2002
Originally published in Great Britain 2002
By Little Tiger Press, An imprint of Magi Publications
Text © 2002 Julie Sykes
Illustrations © 2002 Tim Warnes
Printed in Belgium
1 3 5 7 9 10 8 6 4 2

Library of Congress Cataloging-in-Publication Data

Sykes, Julie.
  Careful, Santa! / by Julie Sykes ; illustrated by Tim Warnes.
    p. cm.
Summary: Santa Claus has one mishap after another one wild and windy
Christmas Eve, despite warnings from his mouse, his cat, and other animals
to be careful.
  ISBN 1-58925-023-0
  [1. Santa Claus—Fiction. 2. Animals—Fiction. 3. Accidents—Fiction.
4. Christmas—Fiction.] I. Warnes, Tim, ill. II. Title.
PZ7.S98325 Car 2002
[Fic]--dc21
                                    2002002115

Careful, Santa!

by **Julie Sykes**

Illustrated by
Tim Warnes

It was Christmas Eve and Santa was loading presents onto his sleigh. Santa's little mouse was helping, too.

Whoosh! A gust of wind blew Santa's beard straight in his face.

"Ho, ho, ho!" he chuckled. "I can't see what I'm doing!"

"Careful, Santa!" warned Santa's cat. "Don't lose that bag of presents."

"That would be terrible!" Santa agreed, as he carefully placed the bag on the sleigh.

Santa helped his little mouse climb aboard the sleigh.

"Hold on tight!" he boomed. "We're off!"

It was a wild and windy night.

"Oh my!" shouted Santa, as the sleigh rocked this way and that. Suddenly, the bag of presents began to move.

"Careful, Santa!" called Santa's little mouse. "Watch those presents!"

But Santa wasn't quick enough. The bag of presents slid across the sleigh and toppled overboard.

"Stop!" cried Santa in alarm. "Down, reindeer, down! I've lost all the presents!"

The reindeer struggled
against the wind . . .

and landed as gently as they could.

"Careful, Santa!" they shouted, but it was too late . . .

"Whoops!" cried Santa, landing on his bottom.

Santa scrambled to his feet. The presents were scattered far and wide and he hurried to pick them up. He didn't notice the frozen pond.

"Whee!" cried Santa, as he slid across the ice toward the duck house.

"Careful, Santa!" quacked the ducks.
"You nearly squashed us."
"How awful," said Santa as he picked
up the presents. "Sorry about that.
Has anyone seen my present bag?"

"Here it is!" chattered a squirrel from high in a tree. Santa bravely climbed up, but before he knew it he was stuck in the branches. "Oh, help!" he cried.

"Careful, Santa!"
called the squirrel.
"I am trying to be
careful," said Santa, as he
struggled to get free. Very
slowly, Santa climbed back
down, dropping some
presents as he went.

At the playground, a few presents were lying
under the swings. Santa put them into his bag,
then he spotted some more on the slide.

"Whoosh!" cried Santa, as he zoomed down the slide.

"Careful, Santa, you're going too fast!" warned Santa's cat.

"Eek! I can't stop!" said Santa, as he slid toward
a snowman.

"Sorry, snowman, I didn't mean to bump you," Santa said
as he dusted himself off and popped the last of the presents
into his bag.

"That's it!" he boomed. "It's time to deliver these presents. Ready, mouse?" But where was Santa's mouse? Santa couldn't see her anywhere.

"Oh dear!" he cried. "First I lose my bag of presents, and now I've lost my little mouse. This is horrible."

The ducks, the squirrel, and Santa's cat all crowded around.
"Don't worry, Santa!" they chattered. "She can't be very far.
We'll help you look for her."

Everyone looked for Santa's mouse.

She wasn't in the duck house.

She wasn't on the swings.

She wasn't near the slide or behind the snowman.

Just then, Santa heard a familiar squeak. He shined his flashlight up . . .

and there was his mouse, hanging from a branch in a tree.
"Careful!" warned Santa. "It's far too windy to play up
there. That branch doesn't look too safe to me."

But the mouse was not playing. "I'm stuck," she squeaked. "Please get me down!"

Quickly, Santa took off his jacket and spread it out on the ground. Everyone gathered around and held the coat like a trampoline.

"Hold on tight, everyone, and don't let go!" said Santa.

"Ready, mouse? One, two, three . . . JUMP!"
Mouse jumped, and with a bounce and a plop,
she landed safely on Santa's coat.
"Hooray!" cheered Santa. "Thank you, everyone."

It was time to go. Santa and his mouse
hurried to their sleigh.

"Reindeer, up, up, and away!" cried Santa.
Whoosh! Blew the wind.

"Careful, Santa," called everyone,
as the sleigh rocked this way and that.
"Look after that mouse, and *hold on
tight to those presents!*"